This book is to be returned on or before
the last date stamped below.

First published in 2002 by
SCOTTISH CHILDREN'S PRESS
Unit 13d, Newbattle Abbey Business Annexe,
Newbattle Road, Dalkeith EH22 3LJ
e-mail: info@scottishbooks.com
www.scottishbooks.com

in conjunction with the
ASSOCIATION FOR SCOTTISH LITERARY STUDIES

c/o Department of Scottish History
9 University Gardens, University of Glasgow
Glasgow G12 8QH

The publisher acknowledges subsidy from the
SCOTTISH ARTS COUNCIL
towards the publication of this volume

British Library Cataloguing in Publication Data
A catalogue record for this book is available from the British Library

ISBN: 1 899827 49 8

Cover illustration © copyright Angus Ferguson
Printed and bound by Bell & Bain Ltd, Glasgow

My Mum's a Punk ...

New Stories and Poems

edited by

Theresa Breslin, James McGonigal
and Hamish Whyte

SCOTTISH CHILDREN'S PRESS

contents

Introduction

When somebody new walks into the classroom, or moves into our neighbourhood, the first questions we want to ask are usually 'What's your name?' and 'Where do you come from?' The same questions apply whether the person comes in dressed like a punk or is just wearing ordinary clothes.

Questions about who a person is and the place he or she comes from are closely linked in our minds. Like the word 'neighbourhood', which means both a place and also the set of people who live there, we know that people are shaped by where they grow and by the folk they grow up with, who tend to talk alike and seem to know a lot about each other's lives.

But knowing 'a lot' is not knowing everything. Growing up is partly about realising that some things and thoughts are personal, not everything can be understood fully or quickly, and not much stays unchanged as the years go by. For that reason, growing older can often be amazing or amusing. You can see things from different points of view.

But it is also a puzzling or lonely experience sometimes, when life seems more serious than it used to be.

This is where stories and poems are useful. They let us see how other people are getting on with growing up – how they deal with their pals or parents, how they make difficult decisions, what intrigues them, who they'd really like to be like.

The stories and poems in this book are all new writing, created for young people in Scotland by contemporary Scottish writers. Because they themselves grew up in different parts of Scotland, their writing comes in a variety of accents and dialects. There is work in English too, of course, and a little in Gaelic. Growing up in Scotland today is partly about learning to listen to the experiences we all share, beyond our local ways of describing them.

Wherever you stay, we hope that you enjoy reading this anthology, and that it gives you new things to think or talk about and new people to get to know. If your mum's not a punk, then here is someone's who is! Your worst nightmare? Maybe – or maybe not.

My Mum's a Punk

At first I didn't notice. You don't when you're that
    wee.
She was just my mum and she was just so fine.
She pushed me in my pram down to the shops and
    chippy,
down to the park, and on the roundabouts and swings.
We went to Gran's and Other Gran's, and to my pal's
    way down the street.

Her mum was just the same. That's when it hit me,
    hard.
Not like Gran or Other Gran, or like the lady in the
    shop,
all skirts and perms and make-up. Our mums were
    different.
They'd no hair, just bristles like a hedgehog
and big Doc Marten boots. Then someone told me
    why.

She said, d'you know? – your mum's a punk.

I watched her every day, and stared at other
    mums.
Down at the playgroup there were lots.
Fat mums, thin mums, big and wee and tall
    mums,
in pretty dresses, cuddly jerseys, some in high-
    heeled shoes.
And no one had a pin stuck through her nose,
    'cept my mum.

That's because it's true – my mum's a punk.

She's special. She's got no respect, just tights
    with holes
and safety pins and lots of jeans with rips. She
    even
has a tattooed skull on both her arms. And you
    should see
her lipstick. Yes – it's black! Not pink or red
like Gran's or Other Gran's or like those other
    mums'.

But I don't care. She's my mum and she's
    great.
She's something special and she's all the mum
    I want.
I never lose her in a crowd like all those
    greeting kids
down at the shops. She always stands out
even from a mile. You know the reason why.
    It's easy.

It's because, you know – my mum's a punk.

Brian Johnstone

Wee Grantie

When Ah wis tellin yiz aboot Jaz an his bike that goat stole, Ah mentioned gaun oot tae the country wi Jaz an Billy Wan-fit. Mind Ah tellt yiz about gaun oan wur bikes tae this place wi a rope swing? Wan summer we wis oot ther a few times, but ther wis wan time in particlar Ah mind, an that wis the time Wee Grantie cam wi us. Ye ken whit Grantie's like? Yon's a total eejit. Ah mean, ther's folk that's a bit daft, but Grantie – he wis worse. Ah reckon Grantie went tae extra classes in bein an eejit. He musta had special coachin in bein stupit, fur naebidy could be that daft wi'oot some sorta help. Jaz reckons Grantie wis drapt heid-first ontae a concrete flair when he wis a wean, but Ah don' think even *that* wid explain it. An everywhere ye went he wis ther, giein it 'Wher yiz goin, guys?' an 'Can *Ah* come?' Thanks tae Grantie we wur better than the S.A.S. at takin cover ahin hedges an wa's an parkt motors, aw it took wis sumdy tae shout 'Grantie Alert!' an we were aw fleein in different directions. Jist noo an then yid feel sorry fur Grantie an let him come wi yiz, but gie it ten meenits an ye wur ready fur stranglin him.

Grantie's proablem wis no jist that he couldnae shut up, it wis the total rubbish he spoke every meenit o the day, an the way he wis pure hyper wi it, ye ken whit Ah'm sayin? Like wan day he's sittin ahin us in class an he's gaun oan an oan aboot how ye can copy ten pun notes oan the school photocopier an naebidy'll ken the difference. An Ah'm giein it 'Shut it, Grantie!', but he goes oan an oan, an when wur oot at dinner time he's still jumpin aboot an in ma face an giein it, 'Ye could print hunners o them, Craigie, an yid be rich, nae bother. See if ye done five hunner yid huv . . . ' He'd tae go away an work that yin oot. An see if ye try tae ignore him, he jumps aboot right in front o ye, right in yer face, an he's grabbin yer airm if ye turn away. Big Tam Melville's the worst wi him. The rest o us cannae staun it, but big Tam cracks up. He goes pure mental wi Grantie. Wan day it took fower o us tae pull big Tam aff him. Wur aw gaun tae Tam efter: 'Lissen, Tam, see if he's buggin ye, jist walk away an leave him.' The next day that's exactly whit Tam did. He cam up tae is in the playgrun an says, 'Ah took yer advice lads, Ah jist walked away an left the wee eejit hingin aboot.' Whit he didnae tell us wis he'd hung Grantie up oan a hook in the cloakroom by his collar first. It was ten meenits afore a teacher liftit him doon. Big Tam threatened tae pack in the fitba team when Grantie joined. We'd a helluva joab persuadin him tae stay, but Tam's a key defender an we couldnae dae wi'oot him.

Gie him his due, Tam tried tae keep the heid wi Grantie, but ye could see he wis strainin at times. Like wan day efter a gemme an wur in the dressin room an Grantie's gaun oan aboot this lassie Karen Aitchison. Noo, tae pit ye in the picture, Karen Aitchison is pure *lovely*. She's in the year above us an she's a total *goddess*. She's gaun oot wi a boy that's left school, he's goat his ain motor an that. Ah mean, Karen Aitchison could walk oan watter an no get her feet wet, ken whit Ah'm sayin? Onyway, Grantie thinks she's secretly in love wi him, an he's goat aw sorta reasons fur thinkin this, an he's sittin ther giein it, 'Ye want tae a seen the look she gied us ootside the chippie,' an, 'Ah think she pure fancies us.' First we try tae mak a fool o him, an when that doesnae work (fur how d'ye mak an eejit o an eejit?) wur tryin tae ignore him an talk among oorsels, an Grantie jist sterts talkin louder an louder. An Ah sees big Tam, an his eyes is sterrin at Grantie an his knuckles is aw clenched an white, an he's daein the heavy breathin, an ye kin jist tell whit's comin next. Ah nudges Jaz an points tae Tam. Jaz sees whit's happenin an huckles Grantie intae the showers. Jaz turns oan the cauld watter an pushes Grantie unner it, claes an aw, an we leave Grantie greetin an go back tae the ithers.

'He needit a cauld shower tae cool him doon a bit. He wis gettin a bit overheatit aboot big Karen,' says Jaz.

Even Tam wis smilin. Ah reckon Jaz had done Grantie a big favour, like.

See if yer thinkin wur awfy hard oan Wee Grantie, it's no' really true. Wan night me an Jaz is doon the Sheepie wi wur bikes an we get talkin aboot Grantie – Ah think it wis the day Grantie had managed tae turn the fire extinguisher oan himsel – an we felt kinna sorry fur the wee guy. Jaz teks us by surprise at times wi how much he kens aboot folk. He does a lot mair thinkin than maist folk realise, he's a right smart yin.

He says, 'Ah ken where Grantie's comin fae, Craigie. See yon time he dragged us back tae his hoose, ye ken how his wee sister has yon condition, spina . . . spina somethin, an she cannae dae much fur hersel, see wi Grantie's parents, it's as if Grantie isnae ther, like he disnae exist. Aw they dae is fuss ower his wee sister, ther no interestit in Grantie.'

'Nae wunner,' Ah says, and we wur laughin an that, but we baith felt a wee bit sorry fur Grantie. Fur twa meenits, that is, an then he arrived, showin aff an yammerin oan an tellin us aboot the time he jumpt right ower twa cars oan his bike, an we wur crackin up at him again. Ah'll bet ye the maist patient person in the world, mibby a nun or somethin, wouldnae last five meenits in a room wi Grantie wi'oot smackin him wan.

Onyway, Ah'm gettin a bit aff the track here, Ah wis gaun tae tell yiz aboot yon day in the country wi wur bikes. The place we wur gaun tae is aboot five mile fae the toon, oot the Stenton road. We planned it the day afore, me an Jaz an Billy Wan-fit, an we wur away afore nine wi wur pieces an stuff. An wur jist passin the fire station an who appears beltin roon the coarner oan his bike? Aye, Grantie. He does this kinna skid turn, faws aff, picks himsel up an says . . . aye, yiv guessed it,

'Wher yiz gaun guys?'

'Naewher special,' says Billy.

'Can *Ah* come?'

Naebody says 'Aye', but he cams onyway. Ah couldnae believe it! The five mile oot tae the swing tree wis like the Toordy France, me an Jaz an Billy tryin tae race oan ahead an Wee Grantie pedallin like a fiend tryin tae keep up wi us. We couldnae shake him aff fur he wisnae fur giein up. By the time we goat ther we kent we'd jist huv tae pit up wi him. He's giein it:

'Why've we stoapt here? Whit we daein? Wher yiz gaun? Whit's ther tae dae here? Yiz bin here afore? How dae yiz ken this place?' an aw that, an wur jist tryin tae ignore him.

Wher the swing tree is cannae be seen fae the road, yiv goat tae go ower a gate, across a field then doon intae this wee valley, like, wi a burn an lotsa big trees. Ther's this big chessie tree wi a rope hingin fae it, an if ye swing oot fae the side o the valley yer right ower this deep pool in the stream. It's pure brilliant – ye get a real buzz swingin oot ther, an the pool's deep enough furra swim if ye want tae cool aff. The three o us hud bin ther a few times, an Ah wis the record holder fur the longest swing. Wee Grantie wis jibberin as soon as he goat ther. We stertit windin him up. Ah says, 'See that big rock ther, Grantie – wan time wur oot here ther wi these ither boys, an wan o them faws aff the rope an splats intae that rock. They'd tae scrape him aff an tak the bits hame tae his maw in a bag.' An Grantie's lookin no' very sure aboot swingin oan it. The three o us wur giein it laldy, swingin oot as high an wide as we could, but Grantie wis a bit kinna careful. Onyway, we mucked aboot fur ages, then we went doon tae the burn an hud wur pieces. Grantie wis gettin mair an mair annoyin, an we wur stertin tae get really sick o him. He's giein it aw yon, 'Bet Ah could catch hunners a fish in ther,' an 'See when Ah wis at the baths last week Ah held ma breath unner watter fur fifteen meenits.' So when he says, 'Ah think Ah'll go in furra swim,' Jaz gies us this wee look an says,

'Aye Grantie, great idea. As long as ye don' mind if the rest o us don' go in, we're gaun back up tae the tree . . . '

An Grantie goes, 'Aye – nae bother, Jaz.'

'But mind ye'll huv tae strip aff, Grantie,' says Jaz, 'fur ye cannae cycle aw the way hame in wet claes – but dinnae worry, naebody ever cams doon here.'

Ah kent this wisnae true, an Ah wunnert why Jaz wis sayin it, but Jaz is giein us a wink, so Ah shuts up.

'Aye – right ye ur, Jaz.'

Ah bet ye can guess whit Jaz does next. It wis brilliant, so it wis – whit a laugh. He waits till Grantie's in the watter an splashin aboot, then he sneaks doon an grabs Grantie's claes – aw o them. Ah mean, it couldnae a worked oot better. Even Jaz didnae ken that they lassies wid arrive! These lassies fae oor school go oot tae a ferm near ther tae dae horse ridin, an sometimes they come ower tae the swing tree afore gaun hame. We hear ther voices, like, an Jaz climbs up the bank an sees the fower o them comin across the field, an he's killin himsel laughin. He shouts 'Grantie – yid better get oot an get yer claes, ther's lassies comin . . . wan o them looks like Karen Aitchison . . . ' An Grantie loups oot the pool like a scerd rabbit an runs fur his claes, but his claes urnae ther. The voices is gettin closer, so he jumps back intae the pool. Jaz signals tae me an Billy tae hide. When the lassies arrive ther's naebody ther except Grantie, cowerin in the scud in the pool. Ther aw gigglin an that, an – an this made it perfeck – they sit doon aside the pool an shout 'Hi, Grantie, want tae come oot an talk tae us?' Grantie wis blushin that much Ah thought the watter wid bile. That's jist fur the first twenty meenits but, fur efter that he musta got caulder an caulder – ye could practically hear his teeth chatterin. He's scuffin up the mud at the boattom o the pool tae try an mak the watter cloudy, but it's no' really workin. Wur still in the bushes guttin wursels, an Grantie's gettin mair an mair frantic. He's shoutin tae us, 'Jaz? Craigie? Billy? – ur ye ther?' The lassies is giein him some slaggin. Finally we stert tae feel a wee bit sorry fur him. Jaz cams oot the bushes haudin Grantie's claes, he says 'Hey Grantie – Ah jist caught a wee dug wi these in its mooth, ther no' yours, ur they?' An Grantie's near greetin by this time.

The lassies finally head back tae the ferm tae get ther lift hame, an when they leave thur kiddin Grantie oan ther gaun tae report him tae the polis. Grantie crawls oot the watter, blue wi cauld an rid wi embarrassment, an we faw aboot laughin again. Grantie's lookin pure confused.

Yer probly expectin me tae say somethin like we felt sorry fur Wee Grantie an we wur dead nice tae him oan the way hame? Well, we wur, but it only lastit aboot five meenits. Then Grantie sterts aw this 'They lassies wur desperate tae see ma boady' stuff. 'They couldnae wait fur me tae cam oot the watter tae get a guid look at us . . . '

An that wis it, nae mair sympathy. Billy sterts 'Last time Ah saw a perra legs like *yours* Grantie, they were haudin up a chicken,' an Jaz an me cannae wait tae join in, whit a slaggin we gied him.

An that's the thing wi Grantie. Even when yur feelin sorry fur him, an mindin how naebody kin be bothert wi him, he goes an ruins it wi aw the rubbish he talks an aw his jumpin aboot an annoyin ye, an then ye lose the heid wi him. It kin be pure brilliant fun windin him up but.

Iain Mills

FOOTBALL HAIKU

FEATHERED
WINGED
FLIGHTED

KEEPER
POACHER
FOWLER

AROUND
THE
GROUND

PARK
UNTIL
DARK

Alec Finlay

Tigger

I know Tigger's no the most original name for a cat, but I was only eight when I got him. I'd really wanted a dog but Mum and Dad said we'd nae room and it wouldnae be fair tae get wan. And a dog would be a lot of work too. I didnae know that my Mum was gonnae have my wee brother then, of course. Danny. He's three now.

Tigger's three and a half but wan year of a cat's life is like seven years of a human's so that makes him twenty-two-and-a-half-year auld. He's orange and stripy and has big long legs, just like Tigger in the cartoon. He's no like other cats. He's a bit wild, likes tae go hunting outside; sometimes he's away all day, but he always comes hame. I put his food down for him just before we have wur tea, then I go oot the back and whistle, a special whistle only I can dae; and he just appears, from naewhere. I don't know any other cats that dae that.

And every night he sleeps on my bed curled up at the bottom, purring away.

When I first got him he was six week auld, a wee bundle of orange fur wi big yellow eyes. Mum tried tae make him sleep downstair. She got a bed for him and put in a hot-water bottle and an alarm clock wrapped up in a blanket. That's supposed tae make the kitten think it's his mother's heartbeat. But Tigger wasnae having any of that. He kept coming up the stair, trying tae get intae my room. He shouted at the door. I don't mean mewed or yowled or any of the normal things cats dae; I mean he shouted, just like a person. Then when nothing happened he started throwing hisself at the door, really throwing hisself hard and scratching wi his claws on the way down, like a cartoon cat. And he never got fed up wi it; he went on and on and on till finally Mum had tae gie in and let him sleep in my room. A lot of folk think that cats are no as good as dogs; they don't dae tricks and they're kind of girlie pets, but Tigger's no like that. He's wild like a dog but he's my cat cause he only comes for me. He's my best pal.

And now Mum wants me tae get rid of him.

It was yesterday she tellt me. It would of been bad enough but I wisht she hadnae done it that way. See, she took me oot for my tea, just me and her, tae the cafe. We used tae dae that when I was wee, afore Danny came along, once a week when my Dad was working shifts and wasnae always hame at teatime. It was our special treat she always said. We'd have egg and chips and tattie scones and I had beans too but Mum doesnae like them. Anyway we never went for a while efter Danny was born cause it was too much bother she said, then when we started tae go again it wasnae the same cause Danny's always stealing my chips – even though he has a plate of his own he always wants mines. I dae mair things with my Dad on my ain noo; he takes me tae the footie and we go fishing sometimes.

Anyhow, when Mum and me went tae the cafe last night it was dead good; just the two of us, sitting in the windae without Danny gaun on and on every time a truck or a bus went by, or chucking his food about. The cafe was warm and noisy and when we'd finished wur food Mum said, 'I want tae talk tae you about something important, Joe.'

I looked at her face, wondering what was coming next. I thought for a minute she was gonnae tell me she was having another baby, but she looked so serious I knew it couldnae be that.

'It's about Danny.'

'Danny? Is something wrang?'

Danny had been gaun for tests at the hospital for a few month now. He gets hay fever and has eczema on his skin too. The doctors were trying tae find oot what was causing it.

Mum said, 'The doctors think he might be allergic tae something. If you're allergic tae something you have reactions tae it, maybe a rash or being sick. It can be something ordinary that doesnae affect most people.'

My Mum sometimes explains things tae me as if I'm five.

'I know what allergic means, Mum. David McSween's allergic tae peanuts – he comes oot in big lumps if he even touches wan. He has tae carry adrenaline about wi him in case he eats wan by accident.'

'That's terrible. Danny's no as bad as that, thank goodness. But the doctors have said he has tae stop drinking milk and eating cheese.'

Danny won't like that. He's practically addicted tae thae wee cheese triangles, the ones that come wrapped up in silver foil. He spreads them on his toast in the morning and puts marmalade on top – yeuch.

'And there's a few other things too. Like Tigger.'

'Tigger?'

'See, they think that Tigger's fur could be affecting Danny – well, no his fur exactly, just some wee mites that live in it.'

I was furious. 'Tigger doesnae have fleas. He wears a flea collar, I gie him that flea powder every summer. And he's the cleanest cat you ever seen. He's always washing hisself.'

'Joe, it's nothing tae dae wi being clean. All cats have wee insects that live in their fur – they're that toty you cannae see them, and normally they don't dae any harm. But some people, like Danny, are affected by them. So I'm asking you tae help oot with this. For Danny.'

Just then, my ice cream arrived; vanilla, wi a flake and raspberry sauce. My favourite. I put the spoon intae the ice cream but it was still quite hard. I only managed tae get a wee bit on the spoon. I put it on my tongue, letting it melt there.

'It's OK, Mum. I'll keep Tigger oot of Danny's way. I could feed him outside and no let him into the house except at night-time. And I'll wait tae Danny's in his bed and carry him up the stairs tae my room. Danny doesnae need tae have anything tae dae wi him.'

Mum stirred her coffee. 'Joe, I'm sorry, son, I don't think that'll be enough.'

'What?'

'I'm asking you tae let us find a new hame for Tigger.'

The ice cream tasted sour in my mouth, like milk that's gone off. I didnae know whit tae say. Mum reached over the table and touched my airm.

'It's OK son, you don't have tae decide just now. And I'm no gonnae force you. It's your decision.'

When we got hame Danny was sitting in his pyjamas, watching a video, haudin his teddy, the special wan he takes tae bed. He used tae have loads of cuddlies; he'd fill the bed wi hedgehogs and bunnies and all sorts, but the doctor said they might be causing the allergies so now he's only got wan. When Mum came in he ran tae her and she lifted him and cairried him up the stair tae his bed. His pyjamas rode up tae the knee and I could see the red patches on his legs, sore and weeping. He has special ointment tae put on it but it's still really itchy and horrible.

Dad was in the kitchen washing up and came tae the door with a tea towel in his hand.

'OK, Joe?'

'Aye, fine, Dad.'

'Enjoy your tea?'

'Yeah. Did Tigger get his?'

'About an hour ago. He's away oot again.'

I went tae the back door and whistled, my special whistle. It was starting tae get dark and the shadows at the back of the garden flickered as if they were alive. I kept thinking I could see Tigger but it it was the light tricking my eyes. I whistled again. Sometimes it took him a while tae get back from wherever he'd been. A wee yowl, a soft shape against my leg and there he was. I picked him up and he rubbed hisself round my neck, purring, his throat vibrating.

That night I lay awake in my bed, Tigger asleep at my feet, as usual. I couldnae imagine what it would be like no tae have him there – a couple of times he'd stayed out all night and I couldnae sleep; no really worried about him cause he's the kind of cat who can take care of hisself, just no feeling right if I couldnae hear his breathing in the night or see his faint outline in the dark at the foot of the bed. And what would it be like no tae wake up wi him licking my face or watch him come hame when I whistle for him?

It would be different if Danny was gonnae die or

something. I know that sounds terrible, but I saw a video once about a boy who gave up one of his kidneys for his brother and if Mum had asked me tae dae that I wouldnae even think about it – I'd dae it right away. I mean you only need wan kidney. And tae see your brother having tae get wired up tae a machine three days a week and no be able tae dae anything, well, that's terrible. But Danny's no seriously ill. I mean he gets a bit stuffed up and his eyes run and all that, but that happens tae loads of folk. And I know eczema's horrible and sometimes he cries because it's sore, but still, it's no fair tae ask me tae get rid of Tigger. I bet they wouldnae ask him tae dae it.

What was it Mum had said? 'I won't force you. It's your decision.' How can I make a decision like that? I wisht she'd just said we're getting rid of him, then I wouldnae have tae decide. I could just blame them. But then, I wouldnae have Tigger.

I moved myself round in the bed so I was lying with my heid at the foot of it, just beside him. I put my foreheid against his back and felt his soft fur, tickly against my nose. Tigger always smells of outside, of grass and earth and leaves. He never opened his eyes but he jerked a bit in his sleep and started tae purr, loudly, his whole body vibrating against my heid.

Maybe I could just wait, see if this no drinking milk helps Danny, maybe I could keep Tigger outside; he could sleep in the shed. At least I'd know he was there, close by. Maybe that would be enough.

Anne Donovan

A Bedtime Story

See thae jeckits? The big puffy silver anes like yer
brither wears? Ehh. The ane that maks him look like a
cross between the First Man on the Moon an the
Michelin man? Well, when eh wiz a laddie in the Ferry
eh hud ane like that. Except it wiz a special jeckit. A
very special jeckit. Ye know how thae jeckits like yer
brither's are made up o different sections, wi stitchin in
between, so's the sections puff up braa an firm between
the stitches? Mine wiz kindo like that, but we didnae
hae the sort of fillin they stuff the modern jeckits up wi.
Naw. Meh jeckit wiz full o air. Ehh. Air. Ye hud tae
blaah the jeckit up. It started as a shrivelled-up lump o
wrinkled plastic, but when ye examined the garment
closely ye discovered that each section had its own wee
tab that ye pulled out tae reveal a clear plastic valve. Ehh.
That's right. Juist like the wee valve on each section o

yer paddlin pool, son. Except that it wiz yer jeckit that wiz covered in valves – aboot twelve o them. So ye'd open each valve up carefully between yer thumb an forefinger, blaah the section fuhl o breath an try an replace the tab intae the wee airtube before any air escaped, so's tae keep each section nice an hard. Mind you, the catch wiz ye'd need so much air that beh the time ye'd managed tae get a sleeve inflated ye'd be blue in the face, gaspin fur air an maybe even hallucinatin, as happened once or twice wi me. So, as ye can imagine, an entire jeckit could take mebbee a hail efternoon tae inflate on yer own. However, if ye had a good team o pals like me, ye'd get them tae help. Wan laddie wid blaw up each section an it wid be a fine sight – a dizzen laddies puffin an blawing at a lump o plastic magically forming intae a jeckit, which ye would ceremonially put on when it wiz half-inflated. It's amazing whut ye could achieve through teamwork an co-operation. Later on, the same laddies frantically heavin an pechin wi bicycle pumps would speed up the process an cut down on effort.

Eh wiz the first in the Ferry wi the jeckit. Efter that aa the ithers got ane tae. Eventually, though, the gimmick wore aff an folk started tae abuse their jeckits, sometimes over-inflatin them till they burst. Ye'd get ten laddies walkin down the road wi their jeckits aa hard an bouncy, makin big squeekin sounds wi the rubbin o the plastic. Occasionally, ye'd get a noise like a great sigh when somebody battered in tae a harled waa too hard an the jeckit burst. Sometimes two of ye wid charge at ane anither wearin over-inflated anes, an ye'd collide wi a thump an bounce back aboot six feet. One time, Boab – him they call The Creator nowadays – got a shot o the foot pump his auld man yaized fur the tyres o his articulated lorry. Eifter Boab accidentally burst six jeckits, he got the hang o the thing and wiz able tae use it tae blaw up tae juist under burstin point, so the jeckit wiz incredibly hard and near spherical. Boab wiz stood there surrounded wi this thing like an inflated straight-jeckit an he suggested that we should see what would happen if each o us could puncture a section at the same instant. When each of us, at the count of three, stuck a pin intae a section o the jeckit, there wiz a great hiss o air. Boab suddenly shot backwards an his feet lifted a few inches aff the ground. Boab wiz slightly shaken an a bit pale, but the rest o us werenae impressed. Afterwards, Boab juist stood there thinking, eyes narrowed, looking at Tam, the weest one o us, but no saying anything. The next day Boab turned up wi a cylinder o helium, complete wi a hose an nozzle, that his big brither got fur him out the British Oxygen yard where he worked. Now Tam wiznae very happy about what Boab suggested, but he wiz wee an light and that's what Boab required for the experiment. Besides, Tam being the youngest, he didnae understand about helium. Helium? That's what they fill the balloons wi at the Carnival, like the wan you let go last summer. Aye – the big silver wan that shot straight up intae the air, over the rooftops an away over the river tae Fife. Boab had once tried an experiment involvin his cat, which he let go of efter he hud tied six helium balloons tae it. I can remember his wee brother greetin as his cat floated out the garden, intae the street, across the road an away out o sight. Well, it took a lot o reassurin Tam that July day doon the beach, but once we convinced him that we would be holding on to a ten-feet rope, he wiz a bit happier. We really meant tae hold on tae the rope, but, ach, we were laddies the same age as you an curiosity got the better o us. What happened? I wiz busy workin the valve o the helium cylinder, inflatin Tam's jeckit which wiz growin bigger an nearin burstin point. At this stage, Boab decided it would be wise tae grab Tam's legs, an I could see he wiz strugglin tae keep him doon. Anither laddie saw this an grabbed the length o rope that had been tied roond Tam's feet. Boab suddenly let go an Tam started tae float slowly upwards an quickly the rope went tight. Next thing the laddie holding the rope started tae leave the ground tae, an half a dozen o us made a breenge fur him, grabbin on tae his feet. I dinnae suppose anybody meant any harm, but when Boab whispered 'let go!' Tam floated up over the beach, gently driftin over the sea, and I'll say this fur him – there wiznae as much as a peep oot the laddie. But we started tae panic when we thought o what we would say tae his Granny who wiz lookin efter him durin the school holidays. While we were making up our minds, Tam wiz floatin further over the Tay, then across tae the North Sea, an ended up in Scandinavia . . . naw! I'm exaggeratin. That's no true. What really happened was that Archie, him that ended up livin wi the Eskimo, kept a cool heid and alerted the Broughty Ferry Lifeboat crew. They put the boat out, sent up a flare, puncturin Tam's jeckit wi the first shot. Tam dropped oot the sky like a shot bird an for a while efter some o the laddies called him Icarus Broon. By the time he wiz picked up in the dinghy, he wiz floatin in the still half-inflated jeckit. Later on Tam became a great sailor, attaining the rank o Submarine Commander. Ye can still see the jeckit in Broughty Castle Museum, wi the big ragged hole made in it by the flare, wi the melted plastic aw aroond it. The press cuttins an photos are there too. I'll take you tae see it on Setterday if ye like.

Aye. Kind o like yer big brither's jeckit.

Night, son.

Bill Duncan

Davie's Story

I wid be about eleeven year auld when I wis prenticed tae the shepherds that workit the hills ahint the wee huddle o houses that wis oor village.

Ma Faither wis determint on it. He said nae son o his wis going to follow his trade – an Innkeeper's life wis nae life at a. Up at the crack o dawn to get the folk fed: hardly tae yir ain bed when it wis time for up again. A'body's servant, wi nae time fir wife or bairns.

'Na, laddie, ye'll be far better aff wi auld Simon an the ithers. Plenty fresh air – the chance maybe o a quiet kip noo an then. An mak nae mistake, bleatin sheep's a pleasanter soun than menfolk bleatin!'

Sae aff I went come the Spring, when they needit mair hauns fir the lambin. I kent I'd miss ma Mither sair, an Faither, an wee sister. An so I did. But auld Simon couldna hae been kinder tae me – he wis mair like a grandfaither. He kept me by him maist days at the start, learnin me a his skilly weys; an if athing was quiet like on the hill, he whiles would send me hame on some ploy atween him an ma faither. Leastweys, that's what he said.

But I kent fine it wis tae let ma Mither see me noo an then, fir she missed me sair an a.

Efter a while, I likit it quite weel; an efter seeven-echt months I thocht it wis jist grand! I learnt how tae tally, an tae fauld the sheep; an whitna kin o herbs and oils tae use on the beasties gin they were hurtit. Efter a while, Simon gied me twa-three sheep fir ma verra ain responsibility, an it was taen fir granted that he wid be keepin me on. Faither an Mither were that pleased, an so wis I! Trampin free on the hill – cooriein aneath a sun-warmed boulder – whistlin when ye liked – singin when ye liked – drinkin in a yer een cid haud, frae the lift above an the valley ablow.

It wis a hard life too, mind, an sometimes the rain an the snell wind were hard tae thole. Lonely, sometimes. Though me jist being a lad, Simon nivir sent me oot o earshot o anither shepherd. At nicht, when the sheep were settled, abody foregaithert roon by Simon's fauld, an the storytellin began. Mony's the time it went on a nicht – or sae they tellt me. But fresh air and weary limbs an a place close by the fire mak fir a sleepy laddie, an maist nichts the stories were hardly begun than I was sleepin soon.

An that's jist whit happened the nicht I missed it a.

The nicht I slept sae soun that Simon had to fairly shake me awake the naist morn. I wis still yawnin, tousled and a bit doited when Simon spak. 'Up wi ye, laddie. Nae sheep fir ye the day. Yir needed at yir ain hame fir a while. Yir mither is run aff her feet wi folk in a the rooms, an yir faither needs anither pair o hauns. Aff ye rin, quick, afore the hale wide world is chappin to get in.'

Simon had me up on my feet by noo, and wis near pushin me doon the track. I tak the hint an stairtit tae rin, when he cried me back – 'Oh, an mind this, laddie, ye're tae gae straucht oot the back, tae the byre.'

'Richt,' says I, an began tae rin again, my mind already on the milkin, when Simon's voice stoppt me a second time. 'Oh, an I think, laddie, it wid be fittin if ye were tae kneel.'

Kneel? Kneel?! Ma Faither said kneelin wis only fir praying or fir greetin some awfy grand body, like a King. Whit wid I want wi kneelin amang the kye?

Which is jist whit I shouted back tae Simon. 'Whit wid I want wi kneelin amang the kye?'

Simon smiled. 'Ye'll fin oot when ye get there, lad.'

An so I did.

Margaret Tollick

Mhairi's Sang

They wir awfy braw an awfy grand
Three strangers frae afar
Speirin at ma faither
Fir a baby an a star.

Faither couldna unnerstaun
I kent fine by his face.
'I canna think that royalty
Wid bide in sic a place.

Folk cryin oot fir wine an breid,
Folk dossin on the flair?
I canna stop tae listen!'
Then he showed them ower the door.

I wis rinnin fir ma mither
Fetchin blankets, servin wine,
When o a sudden sic a thocht
Cam bleezin tae ma mind!

Fir I minded o the lassie
An her man, in oor oot-bye
An the bairnie in the barrie-coat
That times deeved us wi his cry.

Ma mither thocht I'd gone clean daft
When I drappit a, an ran
Tae try an find thae strangers
'Fore they moved their caravan.

They must hae thocht me daft an a
As they stood aboot their fire –
A wee lassie, rinnin, screechin
'It's thon laddie in oor byre!'

Margaret Tollick

Bumble

The vet would like to win the Nobel prize.

I know that he's half-way there already, and I believe, I truly believe, he's going to make it.

As for Bumble the cat, she's well on the way to sanctification. She has never been what she appears to be because she shimmers silvery-grey, but when you run a finger the wrong way through her long fur, she turns up white, pure virginal white, under the silver. Tipped, they say. Tipped for glory.

It was only a hood, because she'd pulled some of her stitches out. A lampshade he called it, when he gave her back. Well, most of her. He kept her leg. Her front left leg. I don't know whether it was partly as a relic, a sacred cat's paw, but it was also for the biopsy.

She did have cancer, which has a nasty habit of killing. But now she doesn't, which is the first kind of a miracle. I thought that, at fifteen, she'd had her nine lives. I still do, what with the time she'd knocked herself out, running into the chair-leg while chasing a green foil ball. Then there was the time she fell asleep on the edge of the table. She sprawled off into the grid of the gas fire and smouldered for a bit. The smell of singed fur filled the kitchen. And the time she couldn't stop sneezing and sneezing and sneezing.

But it was only when she came home again that things became obvious. I didn't quite see it at first and was simply appalled when she jumped out the box, catching her wound, her newly re-stitched wound, on the rim. And there, spreading on her ruined white chest, was this stain, this bright red heart-shaped stain, like a medallion, slung from the crude chain of blue nylon stitches which ran round the shaved half of her neck.

Her hood is kind of cute, really. And a bit of a nuisance. She hasn't quite found her feet, her remaining feet, yet, and open spaces scare her, so she veers to right hand walls and walks along them. She has to slump down for frequent rests, but she keeps her hooded head up.

This is much luckier than a black cat simply crossing your path. This is a miracle cat walking a sacred ring of protection around you. Except that her hood catches on the doorways. It's clear, fine polythene and just a bit wider than her sickles of whiskers. And secured with a fetching strip of white bandage tied in a bow under her chin.

It's a good hood because it stops her chewing her stitches, and bad, because it shoves the food dish along the floor in front of her when she reaches out towards her food.

But when the sun shines on her, as it does in a big beam coming straight down from heaven and falling in a golden pool around her, you can see not a feline Little Bo Peep in her country bonnet, although there is undeniably an element of that, but the angel cat that she is, with her halo finally made visible.

She is much closer to heaven now than she was before. She is lighter, and having only three legs, she touches the ground less.

She is beginning to develop her wings too, which she will need when the time comes for her to fly up to heaven. Her one remaining shoulder-blade is rising up, above her spine and I know it's only a matter of time before the curved case breaks open, probably in the morning sunlight before I get up, and there she will be, like a new dragonfly, proudly pumping up her wings.

But the best bit, which I've been keeping till last, is that I believe, I truly believe, she's growing a new leg. Yes, her fur is growing back, and the scar is ridging over, but I'm sure I can feel something else. As sure as I am about her wings.

I can feel a little lump, just a tiny protuberance, and just under her scar. I believe, I truly believe, this is her new leg. It will be such a transformation. I wonder if the claws will be first or last. I've never seen a leg grow before. Will it be a paw, a lucky paw like a tiny furry bud, which will flower into pads and claws? Will it have fur from the start, or will it be bald, like her shaved bit? I'll know soon.

I haven't dared to share the news with the vet yet. Not until I'm sure. I wouldn't want him to get over-excited about his Nobel prize. I'll wait until it's big enough to be indisputably a new paw and then I'll introduce Bumble of the Ten Lives, Bumble of the Sacred Bleeding Heart, Bumble the Winged Angel Cat.

Bumble, the Patron Saint of All Cancer Sufferers, joint Nobel laureate with the vet.

Valerie Thornton

Naebodie blethers in Scots

ay, A dae	dae ye nou?
ay, A do	dae ye now?
ay, I do	dae you now?
yes, I do	do you now?
yes, I dae	do you nou?
yes, A dae	do ye nou?
ay, A dae	dae ye nou?
ay, A aye dae	nou ye dae
aawhyles, ay	ay, aawhyles
dae you?	ay, A dae tae!

Liz Niven and **Pete Fortune**

SKELP

Whin ah wis wee
ye goat a skelp
if ye didnae dae
whit ye wur telt.
Fair made ye yelp,
a skelp ye felt –
a scud oan the lug
or oneywhere
yer skin wis bare.
Scud or skelp,
ye didnae care
whit they cried it.
It wis *sair*!

Janet Paisley

SKITE

Banana skins ur slippy flairs
kin make ye skite an faw.
Ye kin skite oan ice ur snaw
an that's no aw.
If somedy shoves ye
ye kin skite *aff* a waw.
Whit's mair, if yer mither says
'Ah'll skite ma haun aff yer jaw'
run, cause that's sair an aw.

Janet Paisley

SAUN

Ye cannae staun
in saun,
cannae git gaun.
It gits in yer claes
an atween yer taes,
steys there fur days
bit rins oot yer haun.
Ah cannae staun
saun.

Janet Paisley

Scotland

Bennachie
Don an Dee

Kent his faither
Grouse 'n' heather

North Sea Ile
Barlinnie Jyle

Irn bru
Rangers blue

Grandpa Broon
Gowf at Troon

Midgies heezin
Salmon season

St Andrew's flag
Muckle stag

Peer man's stovies
Buttered rowies

Dark Culloden
Scarlet rodden

Arbroath smokies
Sweetie pyokies

Robert the Bruce
Harvest Moose

Athole brose
Wee fite rose

Fish 'n' chips
Whisky nips

Shetland seals
Echtsome reels

Nessy's hame
Curler's game

Cairngorm
Hairy sporran

Drivin snaa
Hadrian's Waa

William Wallace
Yowes on Harris

Wee Free Kirk
Heilan stirk

Whuppity Stoorie
Bannocks, floory

Parridge pot
Sir Walter Scott

Burns Sonnet
Tartan bunnet

Buts 'n' bens
Misty glens

Tattie dreel
Herrin creel

Hotch potch
Double scotch

Oor Willie
Jabots, frilly

Fitba match
Herrin catch

Capercailzie
Forkietailie

Granny's sookers
Littlins' dookers

John Knox
Torry Rocks

Largs, Dunblane
Sleet an rain

Glesga Toun
Dingin doon

Princes Street
Dreepin weet

Sheena Blackhall

Dinosaur

A dinosaur! A dinosaur!
We niver saw the like afore!
The beastie makks the bairnies roar
Frae Sumburgh tae Singapore!

A dinosaur! His muckle moo
Has teeth as lang as knives,
An fin he roars, the tabby
Losses aa its seeven lives!

A dinosaur! His ilkie snore
Caas continents ajee.
An fin he piddles lochs arise,
As braid's the Irish Sea.

A dinosaur! Fit dis he ett?
A herd o coos fur tea!
He sweels it doon wi a lagoon
O vats o barley bree.

A dinosaur! His heid's amang
The aeroplanes an stars.
His legs are pylons, tail's as lang's
A traffic jam o cars.

A dinosaur's a fearsome breet
Fin it lies doon tae claw,
Bit fin it daunces, *hae a care*
Skyscrapers stert tae faa!

Sheena Blackhall

Skunk

A skunk on skates, a hairy hunk!
He flashed, he footered, he stank, he slunk.
Grampa leapt out of his bunk
with a doughnut still to dunk.
Mammy slammed the door: 'We're sunk!'
'Would you rather have a monk-
ey?' shrieked the stroppy skunk.
They were all in a blue funk
till Bobby said, 'Give him a chunk
of garbage, that'll knock the spunk
out of him!' Down he went, plunk.
They stashed the guzzler in a trunk.

Edwin Morgan

Big Issue

Tinkie tinkie tarry brikks
Hear the toonsfowk cry,
Dinna staun in oor street
Beggin on the sly.

Brukken teeth an ragnails,
Hauns as thin's a cleuk,
Like a tattiebogle,
Creepit frae a neuk.

Hooded een an flechy sark,
Jaiket, walloped wide,
Fa wid let yon coorie
Roon their clean fireside?

Styterin on spinnle shanks,
Twa spurtles weirin sheen,
Sookin frae a bottle,
Oblivion's his frien.

Tinkie tinkie tarry brikks
Seen in ilkie toon
Some ither body's dother
Some ither body's loon.

Sheena Blackhall

THE VISITOR

Hearing there was going to be a special Lucky Dip at Sam's party, Terence punched his fist in the air, 'YES!', then started running up and down the school steps as fast as he could. He ran faster and faster. Not because of the Lucky Dip or the party; not for anything at all, only a sudden need to punch the sky and to keep running up and down the steps until he crashed over. The afternoon heat hit back at him; it felt like he was pounding the sun itself, and couldn't stop . . .

By the time he was in class Terence had calmed down. He sat next to the open window and every so often glanced in the teacher's direction: Macallister was telling them the Earth was a greeny-blue dot that went hurtling through empty space at hundreds of miles per hour; it turned too steadily for anyone to notice – but they would if it stopped, like when someone slammed on the brakes in a car; UFO's and aliens, he added, were nothing but things on TV. Macallister's voice had hit drone-level. The party was going to be in less than three hours. It was good visiting someone else's house, everyone was pleased to see you, and you were pleased to see them. Sam had told him there was going to be a big model ship: red funnels, gangways with tiny stairs, cabins with portholes, and the hold was a Lucky Dip crammed with presents for whoever was invited. Terence had tried to smile: he and his dad didn't bother much about presents anymore.

Hurtling through space or not, there was no sign that the classroom or the village, never mind the whole of planet Earth, was trying very hard to reach four o'clock. Every minute was taking ages: inside – the drone of Macallister's voice; outside – the same single-track road as always, the same fields, the same dykes, hedges, trees, the same river, the same everything. He'd told his dad about Sam's party, told him a week ago, told him every day since, and again last thing before leaving for school this morning. 'Aye, right,' was all the reply he'd got. His dad had never said, 'You're not going,' or 'Party? I'll party you,' which he might well have done. Just, 'Aye, right.' So his dad knew.

To be on the safe side he'd be in the house and out again in seconds – nothing more than a blur of party-best trainers, jeans and 'X-files' T-shirt going up Mosslands Brae before his dad had any idea he'd been home.

They were set to do paired reading: it was Terence's week with the Gom. Time had been crawling along before but right next to the Gom it came to a complete standstill. It was well-known the Gom could hardly do anything for himself, the rumour was that his mother took her pot scourer to his Gom-face once a week. The Gom tried harder than anyone else in class and, wherever they touched, his hands left sweat-marks of effort behind them. When it came his own turn to read, Terence planned to keep well clear of Gom-prints, even if the book did have a plastic cover. He watched the Gom-gaze jerk itself across the page one word at a time:

'The-boy, The-boy-is, The-boy-is-H-, The-boy-is-H . . . '

At this rate even three o'clock was never going to come. All around them the rest of the class was seated in pairs facing each other. There was a steady murmur of reading-aloud. From time to time he could hear Macallister's voice as he went about the room, correcting mistakes. Terence could see the Gom's eyes boring into the page so hard that if the sticky hands let go, the book would probably stay pinned where it was, in mid-air.

'The-boy-is-H-H-'

'Try it a letter at a time,' Terence whispered.

The Gom took a big swallow of air then continued, 'The-boy-is H-O-P-I-N-G – hopping-the D-O-G, the dog.' For the first time since he'd started to read, The Gom looked up: 'Hopping the dog?' He looked utterly lost.

Terence was about to laugh out loud when he saw a large tear roll down the Gom's cheek. 'That's right,' he said quickly, 'the boy's hopping the dog, making it dance, it means maybe. I'll do the next bit.'

He took the book from the Gom, being careful where he put his fingers, and held it right to his face so as not to see the tears the Gom hadn't even sense enough to wipe away.

'The boy is hopping the dog – training it, Gom, teaching it to do tricks, so's it – ' he carried on reading, 'will-catch-rabbits-when-they-go-out-later.' He could hear the Gom sniffling and swallowing, but kept on reading to hurry things along and stop the other boy's misery from getting too close. When he could hear that the Gom was back to normal – Gom-normal, that was – Terence raised his eyes over the top of the book.

'Sam's party's after school. You going?'

The Gom shook his head. 'No.'

'Won't be a big party, I don't think. There'll be a model ship with presents in it.'

'For the sailors?'

The sailors? Trust him to ask a Gom-like question. He closed the book, ready to go back to his own seat. The afternoon was bound to start speeding up once he was safely out of Gom-range.

Shouting goodbye to Sam and the others and saying he'd see them soon, Terence turned left out the school gates to head down Mosslands Brae. He couldn't wait to get to the party, but was in no rush to go home. Blue sky, no clouds, insects buzzing in and out the hedge beside him; he could smell the heat rising from the tarmac road. He stopped, leant against the metal bar of a gate, and looked at some cows standing in the shade.

At once, the sunlight became harsh on his bare arms and on the backs of his hands; it seemed ready, if given half a chance, to gouge its way into his skin. He continued walking, slowly, down the hill.

Bit by bit Mosslands Farm had been sold off until nothing much remained but the farmhouse and outbuildings – peeling paintwork, rotted window frames, rusted gutters, missing slates – a weedy flower-garden in front, weedy vegetable-garden at the back, and two small fields where sheep wandered in and out, stepping over what was left of a wooden gate. When his mother had been alive, strangers driving past sometimes thought it so 'picture-postcard-looking' they'd pull up to take photographs. Visitors had always said what a lovely house it was and how good it must be to live there. Maybe if he pretended to be a visitor himself the house would feel like it used to, and things would go better. Things had always gone better when there was a visitor.

At the turn in the road he crouched down and peered over the stone wall: no sign of his dad in the garden. But sometimes he'd work a bit in the vegetable patch – and, yes, there was his spade sticking out of the ground at the top end of a potato row, and the earth was darker from being dug recently. The yard was empty except for the tractor that hadn't moved in years and some rusted milk churns. Not a breath of wind anywhere, and heat that seemed to nail down everything.

He crept round to the side of the house, and halted: the living-room curtains were closed. He knew what that meant.

But, he reminded himself, he was going to be a visitor today. He'd go in to see this lovely old 'picture-postcard' farmhouse, and this time things would be different from usual.

So, here's the visitor lifting the latch on the gate, easing up the gate-frame a good couple of inches to push it open enough to let himself in. Then up the stone path, past the patches of overgrown lawn on either side and the thick greenery in the flower-beds. What a nice place this is: what a nice garden, flowerbeds and some grass and bushes, and even a nice pump. Never mind the dirt and dryness it coughs up, it looks really old, which was what the visitors had always seemed to like most. The front door's for visitors, it's not locked. He goes in.

Much darker inside, cooler. In the hall he hesitates,

one hand resting on the small wobbly table where the phone used to be. He tries his best to breathe normally. It feels like one of those days when his mother would have rushed up to him: 'Your dad's not well – best not to bother him.' Sometimes he can still hear her voice, still feel her touch.

By now, a real visitor would have lifted his hand from the table and said, 'What a nice table,' then glanced over at the grandfather clock and said, 'What a nice old grandfather clock.' If it had been years ago and his dad in a good mood, the case would have been opened to display the heavy brass pendulum swinging slowly from side to side – so slowly that its Tick . . . Tick . . . Tick . . . seemed always at the point of stopping.

The living-room, the room where visitors are supposed to go, is through the door to his left.

A couple of steps inside the door the visitor pauses: with the curtains pulled it's difficult to see much at first – but he should take his time, visitors are always safe. What a nice room: he can make out the china cabinet, the fireplace with its coal-effect electric fire in front, the TV and video on their trolley. Very nice.

'What are you creeping around for?'

Cold-drenched to the stomach, too afraid to turn round, Terence tried to speak: 'I-was-just- '

'Creeping around. For what?' His dad grabbed him by the shoulder. 'And look at me while I'm talking.'

The sudden shove sent him spinning backwards against one of the armchairs.

Without letting go of the chair-back Terence turned and steadied himself: 'I was just -'

'Creeping in or creeping out – which is it?'

In the dim light, his dad's face seemed a criss-cross of red smudges and blackness where he'd not shaved.

'I'm just in. There's Sam's party and – '

'Just in, are you? And going straight out? That the ticket?'

Terence could feel spittle hitting against his skin but knew better than to wipe it off, he took a step backwards: 'No – '

'No? But you didn't call out, did you? Didn't come round the back as usual, like you'd be expected to, did you?'

With each 'Did you?' his father took a step nearer him, and he took a step further away.

'Time you learnt to behave. And till you do, you're going nowhere.'

'But Sam's party – '

'Only yourself to blame.' His father had reached out and grabbed him by the shirt front: 'Come here.'

He stepped back – and the shirt ripped.

'Now look what you've done, boy.'

A slight breeze made the heat feel like warm breath on his shoulders. He lay quite still, facedown on the field, wanting the heat to melt him away till there was nothing left, nothing but the smell of the grass under him. With a fistful of it in each hand and pressing himself hard against the ground, he felt like he was holding onto planet Earth as it hurtled through empty space – holding on, but only just.

Three things: the heat, the grass, his father's rage; he'd no sense of anything else. He could concentrate on each of them for only so long. It was his dad's rage that kept returning . . .

Finally – ten minutes? half an hour? an hour? he'd no idea – he sat up, wiped his face with his sleeve, pulled his torn shirt over his shoulder and got to his feet.

The house was locked, of course, back door and front. He knocked and shouted. He cried, screamed to be let in. He hammered at the door with his fists, kicked it. A waste of time, like he knew it would be.

The village streets were empty. He walked past the church hall, the pub, the council cottages. No one in sight – they'd all be at Sam's party or having their tea. Where tellies were on, screenfuls of people were the most colourful parts of the rooms he could see into. No telly for him, when the doors were locked at his house they stayed locked a good while.

Then he saw someone. The Gom, looking like a lost Gom and standing nowhere in particular halfway down the low road.

He gave him a wave: 'How's The Gom?'

The Gom waved back and grinned: 'Hello, Terence?' More like a question, but with The Gom you could never be sure.

'It's me, all right. There's nobody else, Gom, just the two of us.' He went up to him: 'With the place empty as this, we can be aliens, like Macallister was saying.'

'How do you mean?'

'Like out of a UFO, visitors from another planet.'

The Gom said nothing for a moment, then looked

around him. 'I belong here.'

Trust The Gom not to get it.

'You and me, we could take over the village right now. You can have everything up to the War Memorial, and I'll have it from there to the river.'

'My gran's waiting for me.' The Gom looked closer at him: 'How come your face's all blood?'

'Don't you want to be an alien? You can come from anywhere in the universe. Anywhere you like.'

'And your shirt's ripped.'

He glared at the red-scoured face: 'See you Gom, you'd make a good alien. A natural. You wouldn't even have to pretend.'

'D'y not want to change it? Or get washed? You could come to my gran's and – '

'Bugger all's what I want, from you, your gran or anybody!' That was the kind of thing his dad said. 'BUGGER ALL!' he yelled, and ran away.

The back door was still locked. He went round to the front – still locked as well. He was hungry and thirsty. He bent down and lifted the flap of the letter-box: an American woman's voice said, 'And so they should be!'

and the studio audience's laughter came booming off the lino floor and the bare walls. He could picture his dad lying at full stretch on the couch, probably still wearing the greasy old boiler suit he never seemed to take off, the colours from the TV screen playing over him. This time he didn't even bother trying to shout or knock.

Next morning, Terence woke to the sound of rain smashing against the skylight window just above his head. He'd slept on the loft floor of the barn. Shivering, he picked the straw from his hair and face, gave his clothes a few slaps to get rid of the dust and sat up. Through the grime and cobwebs he could see low sagging clouds and, in the distance, trees being wrenched from side to side; over by McVey's, the corn had turned into a sea of yellow waves rushing again and again at the hedge-line, trying to break through and flood the neighbouring fields.

The rain streaming down the filthy glass made everything look only half-formed: the stone dykes blackened by the wet seemed to leak into the tarmac road; the birch trees along the river were tangled up with the running water one moment, then blown into the air the next. A real storm.

He got to his feet and brushed the worst of the straw from his clothes. A few moments later he'd climbed down the ladder and was running across the yard in the pouring rain, making for the back door. It was open.

The house was silent except for over by the cooker where a leak splashed onto the lino every couple of seconds. Drip – Drip – Drip. He'd washed his face at the kitchen tap and was drying himself on a tea-towel when he suddenly caught sight of his father through the window. Out in the pouring rain, and not wearing a coat or anything, just the usual boiler suit. He was standing quite still, his hands resting on the spade as if he couldn't decide whether to start digging or not. What was he doing out there? Terence didn't care so long as he got himself well away from the house in time. While keeping watch out the kitchen window he bolted down two Mars bars then a butter-piece and took several large gulps of lemonade. From a heap of clothes lying on the floor waiting to be washed he took a sweatshirt.

Breakfast over, he grabbed his denim jacket and left.

At school everyone was talking about Sam's party and asking why he hadn't been there.

He had his answers ready: 'My dad needed me . . . I was busy . . . There's more to life than parties.'

Sam had brought him his Lucky Dip present from out of the ship – he said thank you and stuffed it in his pocket to open later.

All morning while Macallister's voice droned on and on and on he kept thinking about his dad, and picturing him exactly as he'd seen him earlier: standing out in the garden, gripping onto the spade handle like onto the helm of an old-fashioned ship, and looking like a captain fighting to stay afloat in the middle of a storm. The deck was a pitching, sliding mass of rain, earth, long grass, branches, bushes, torn leaves.

It was during paired-reading with The Gom – he hardly listened, and when it was his turn he just read into himself – that Terence suddenly realised what he had to do.

He'd invite The Gom to his house over lunchtime; he'd be the first visitor they'd had in years. With a visitor, everything would be all right.

The Gom said no, his mum was expecting him home and she'd be worried. She got really worried if he was only five minutes late even.

Let her know then. Sam lived next door to The Gom, and could let his mum know he'd be a bit late. No problem.

But she'd have made something for his lunch and if he didn't –

For some of lunchtime then? He wanted him to come, it would be good fun, the two of them; just for a short time?

The Gom wasn't happy. He sat and sat and said nothing, he seemed to be sweating more than ever.

Terence was standing at the bottom of Mosslands Brae, outside his house. The rain hadn't stopped all morning and was coming down even harder. He'd have to go in. Maybe his dad wouldn't have got back yet, maybe he'd just ignore him.

'Terence?'

His mother? He was afraid to look round.

'Terence?'

A real voice. He mustn't have heard her coming

behind him because of the rain. Then her touch at his sleeve. Ready to throw himself into her arms, he turned round:

'You? What are you doing here, Gom?'

'I–was– '

'You were creeping around.'

'I've come like you asked. Not for long. But you asked me, people don't ask . . . not much.'

Terence gave him a smile.

The Gom smiled back showing his teeth and gums.

Because he was with a visitor today there'd be no need for crouching down and peering over the wall. Straight in the gate, pointing out the lawn, the flowers, the old pump; then through the front door and into the dim-lit hall to show off the small table, the grandfather clock. The Gom kept nodding and smiling. Terence opened the case and let him see the pendulum.

'Needs wound up,' he explained.

Where was his dad? He wanted him to know they had a visitor, then maybe he'd be friendly like he'd sometimes been before . . . offer them lemonade . . . wind up the clock so they could watch the pendulum swing backwards and forwards like it used to, and hear it tick.

His dad wasn't in the living-room either. They looked at the china cabinet, then went through to the kitchen.

'I wanted you to meet my dad.'

'Seen him before, in the village, in the shop, loads of times and – '

After they'd dried themselves off on the tea-towel, Terence poured some lemonade and got out the packet of Mars bars. The Gom kept complaining he'd have to be getting home, his mum would be wondering where he was. Thanks for the lemonade and the chocolate, but he had to go.

'There's something I want to show you, something really special! Something secret!'

The Gom looked desperate: 'Have to go.'

'Only take a few minutes. Honest.'

Terence lead the way out to the back garden. First he walked up the path and pointed to the different vegetables, shouting to be heard above the wind and driving rain: 'These are potatoes . . . onions . . . peas . . . cabbages . . . carrots . . . '

When they reached the top of the rows they'd run out of garden: only a couple of feet of grass, then the dyke, then nothing.

The Gom was pulling at his arm. 'Have to go. Have to go.'

'See this spade – ' Terence began, 'Well, remember Sam's party?' He smiled, 'The ship you heard about? And the hold and the Lucky Dip and everything? Well, my dad's been burying presents for us, for you and me, and – '

But the Gom was already running back down the path: 'Getting late, Getting late.'

'You've got to stay, don't – '

The spade lifted easily out of the ground. Seemed light as a feather almost. He raised it, swung it above his head, aimed in the direction of the vanishing Gom.

Then hurled it as far and as high as he could.

The clang the metal made hitting the stone path felt like a blow in the face. Terence staggered back against the wall. So very, very cold. Chilled suddenly. As if he'd never get warm again, ever . . .

His father was standing at the back door and looking angrier than ever. This was going to be the worst. The very worst.

Terence began walking towards him, slowly. 'There's

been a visitor.'

His father said nothing.

'A visitor. He's gone now. I showed him the house like we used to. The kitchen, the garden and everything.'

He'd almost reached him. 'I did everything right, dad. Gave him something to drink and a Mars.'

'What the hell are you talking about?'

'He needed looking after, the visitor. Been out in the rain and everything. Needed looking after.'

'No visitors wanted in this house, no bugger all wanted. Just you. Get yourself inside.'

Not wanting to risk being hit Terence ran past him through the doorway. 'Dad – '

'Visitor, my arse.'

'He said – he said to say hello to you.'

In the kitchen it was even darker than before, and cold. Rain was gusting hard against the window. His dad sat down.

Terence knew he had to keep talking. 'You're soaked as well, just like him.' He pushed the damp tea-towel within reach. It was ignored. Rainwater continued running off his dad's hands onto the table.

He had to do something. Anything.

Having dug in his pocket he pulled out the present Sam had given him. 'The visitor – he left this for you.'

'What are you on about?'

'A Lucky Dip prize. For you,' he said. 'It's special.' Terence put it on the table and took a step back, 'I'd better be getting to the school. You can open it, if you like.'

'Lucky dip?' His father had picked up the small sellotaped package and was turning it over and over in his wet hands. 'What the hell do I want with a lucky dip?'

Like he'd never seen a present before, thought Terence as he edged further away; like it was something that had dropped from the skies.

He grabbed his jacket and left.

Once outside, he splashed his way across the yard. At the gate he stopped, then turned to look back at the house. He was aware he was getting drenched through, but still he waited. The curtains were closed, water was gushing out of the rones and guttering and running down the front stonework, from nearby came the scrape and screech of corrugated iron being wrenched loose by the wind from one of the sheds, the front garden was turning into mud.

Suddenly he shouted: 'It was an alien that's gone back to his own planet – one visit here was enough for him!' and started laughing.

Next moment he was marching up the road through the wind and rain, stamping through the puddles, swinging his arms at his sides and yelling at the very top of his voice: 'LUCKY DIP! . . . LUCKY DIP! . . . LUCKY DIP!'

Terence would have to go home at some time – but it wouldn't be for hours yet. For the time being he knew he was safe.

Ron Butlin

No Daisies

(for my grandmother)

Arid, this acid soil:
Silver-grey, it whips in the wind
Like ash from dead cigarettes.

The pines have soaked the goodness
From the land
And nothing else grows here:
No grass, no daisies;
Not even the wild pink foxgloves
Whose bells would steal our wishes.

Even the lichen, crusted on your headstone
Has withered: dry and dusty,
It crumbles to my finger
Which traces the weathered letters
Of your name.

Dee Rimbaud

Memories of a War Child

Why are my childhood memories mobbed
  with air-raids, bombs, collapsing houses,
  crashes, fires, and explosions –
  shadowed by fear?

Why are my childhood memories so full
  of empty stomachs,
  bestial foraging for food?

Why are my childhood memories biting with winter
  cold?
  Worn-out rags all day and night,
  each other's warmth the only help on our side.

Why are my childhood memories aflood with tears?
  Women's faded aprons soaked with sadness
  will not fade from my mind.

Why are my childhood memories crowded with
  loneliness?
  My feeble child voice drowned in the clatter of war,
  I stood alone – powerless victim.

Why are there still war children today?

Why?

Ingrid Lees

Children's Bookshop
at Midnight

The shelves are groaning
with books to be read,
but they are all closed
and the children in bed.
Without readers, characters
cannot jump off pages,
must play out their stories
in shut book cages.

Ingrid Lees

Tree Poem

Can you hear the tree's heartbeat
and the slow rustle of its imagination?

Can you feel its wriggling roots
deep in the soil beneath your feet?

Can you hear the silence fall
as it shakes the darkness from its hair?

Can you see it stretch its branches wide
as dawn opens the eye of the sky?

Can you see the tree scratch its rough trunk
and wash its face in the dew?

Can you see the tree dreaming?
Can you hear the leaves breathe?

Can you see the tree seeing you?

Magi Gibson

A Green Thought

It is as green and as curly as new parsley, the number three, and should be loved above all other numbers and letters.

Loved too for its harmonious potential because, when you cross two parsley-green threes, they create the most beautiful bottle-green nine. And before, during and after the calculation, there is such a pleasing intensification of greens. It's an act of generation worth envisaging on a daily basis for the beauty of the shifting green transformation, for its perennial freshness and comforting pervasiveness.

Division, like subtraction, is never as good as combination. Bottle-green divided by parsley results in only one orphaned green three, in a loss of green, an absence of green parents from the process.

To call three times three 'squaring' is to miss the

point. Or rather, to add an extra point, because the basis of three is triangular, not quadrangular. It may work in the flatness of two dimensions, where a square of parsley by parsley units, equals an area of bottle-green squared units, but the result is a small dark lawn crying out for the freedom of the plains and open skies.

This restriction to two dimensions overlooks the green power and triangular essence of threes and nines. Three times three is three triangles, is nine. Its balance is obvious and very pleasing. To suggest that triangles are more akin to addition than multiplication is simply to acknowledge that multiplication is a sophisticated short-circuit for multiple additions of the same number. Only the narrow-minded would assume, however, that all numbers and all calculations are equal.

'Table' is too flat and quadrilateral a name, but nothing surpasses the nine times table for its sheer green virtuosity.

As the nine contains the memory of parsley growing in its past, so the future of the nine times table is ultimately and always green.

All other numbers are mere ciphers, peripheral and disposable, a means to an end. The dark and light blues of six and seven can go, consigned to the winds with the dark red four. The other insipid sandy-coloured, white or clear numbers fade into oblivion. Only three and nine survive and grow.

Thus, bottle-green nine multiplied by china-white two becomes, but briefly, a clear one and a sandy eight. Seduced by the charm of the green numbers, they merge into nine. Similarly with two plus seven, the temporarily ungreen product of bottle-green times parsley. Connoisseurs find nine times thirty-seven especially viridescent . . .

And so with all the nine times table, which glides like a gathering green river, dotted with bright parsley threes, while the detritus of all other numbers is washed up on its banks in the inexorable flow towards the sea of green infinity.

Valerie Thornton

Dream Eclipses Reality

Yesterday I painted
Great big happy faces
On all the skyscrapers
In the Gorbals . . .
And what if skyscrapers
Really did scrape
The sky?
I would attach paintbrushes
Dripping with rainbow colours
To their radio masts
And lightning conductors.

Dee Rimbaud

Blue Phones

we both have
wee blue telephones
my sister and I

we bought them
one in Glasgow, one in Edinburgh
for nine pounds each
rejects from the phone shops
'they don't make them like that anymore'
the woman said
'they're withdrawing the dials'

in the glossy brochure
there are phones
'just perfect for today's lifestyle'
'to complement any décor'
none of them have dials
none of them are blue

but the wee blue phone is dinky
looks like a toy
people think it isn't real
until it rings at them

it sits on the fridge
on top of newspapers and books
or on the kitchen table
among geraniums and cups

my sister's phone
sits on her workbench
staring at tools
or lies on the floor
tangling with balls of wool

when I dial her number
I know how it looks
when she answers
in her room with the violins
on the walls
and she, talking to me
and maybe sipping milky tea
sounds close enough to hug

Elizabeth Burns

Gille-Mirein *Whirligig*

Thàinig tu fhèin air ais
A-steach nam àite
Ri marbh na h-oidhche.
> *You came back*
> *into my place*
> *in the dead of night*

Thog thu a-nuas
An gille-mirein
As a' chiste
'S chuir air ghleus e.
> *you took down the whirligig*
> *out of the kist*
> *and set it spinning*

Bha mi air cuimhne
Chall gu faodadh tu a chur a' crònan, a' seinn –
> *Fancy forgetting*
> *you could make it*
> *sing!*

A-rithist, 'ille!
> *Encore!*

Rody Gorman

Superman II

He plays in his room
With his millennium ball,

All
That yellowbluegreenpurplepinkred

Extended
To the maximum

He presses on it,
It contracts in on itself,

The space
Inbetween
Begins to close in
The whole
Somehow grows less bright.

He places it back on its shelf.

Rody Gorman

The Wire-Mesh Tiger

Its wire-mesh tail in a frozen flick.
It bares wire-mesh teeth,
roars a silent roar

and when the museum's
thick oak doors creak shut
and keys clunk in their locks,
when lights are dimmed
and workers button up to the night

the wire-mesh tiger creaks to life
pads paw-prints
on the carpeted walkway,
feels the cold
of the red sandstone floor

peers through the windowed wall,
under stained glass paintings of
dragons, saints and angels
towards the slumber of Pollok Park.

Cosy in their fields

Highland cattle in long-hair blankets
snuggle on a brown-leaf bed

beside chestnuts knocked to the ground
by playtime daytime children.

The wire-mesh tiger
yawns a wire-mesh yawn
then beds down for *his* night
in an oak four-poster bed.

The wire-mesh tiger
dreams of home and brothers and sisters
in the baking sun and swishing trees.

In the morning's early hours
a bird song alarm
tears the tiger from his dreams.

And as the rays of the fresh sun
sparkle through
a stained glass angel

the wire-mesh tiger of Bandhavgarh
once more resumes its frozen pose,
preparing for visitors of the new day.

The Plaster Tiger

I'm a plaster tiger, woman-made.
I'm muscle and blood.

I'm an earth-brown-red
as if the colour of my heart
has become the whole of me.

I'm surrounded by watercolour brothers
hiding in their artist's jungles.

I have no bones man can use
            to grind into tonic
                        that he thinks cures his head-ache.

I have no whiskers man can use
      to boil into lotion
            that he thinks cures his tooth-ache.
I have no flesh man can use
      to bubble into medicine
            that he thinks cures his belly-ache.

So, for the moment I'm safe,
still, always on my guard.

See how I'm ready
crouching
poised, prepared to pounce, if required,
on *the* most dangerous of animals.

The Watercolour Tiger

When peacocks-blue call
through green jungle vine.

When white cattle and black ibis doze.

When slithery snakes slide
through the undergrowth.

When white-plumed egrets wing to roost.

When chitals first bark
from distant dusky mountains.

When women
with yellow, blue and purple saris
with full baskets balanced on their heads
walk home the dusty road, graceful as deer.

When the rays of the large orange sun
like evening fingers
tuck in the little sleepy village.

The tiger wearing
his orange black-striped coat,
peers through
the brown green and gold
of his tall-grass bamboo curtain

with orange watching eyes.

His ears alert, twitching.
His sharp teeth bared.

Brian Whittingham

Inspired by the 'Wild Tigers of Bandhavgarh'
exhibition at the Burrell Gallery, Glasgow.

Craigie in Love

See when Ah wis wee Ah used tae think aw yon 'love' stuff wis a loada rubbish, aw that haudin hauns an wee kisses in the moonlight an aw yon stuff. Ah widnae a believed Ah could be like that masel. An then Ah met Ellen McGill.

Ellen didnae go tae ma school, she went tae the ither yin ower at Heathcroft. Ah wis up ther wi Jaz wan night efter the fitba, jist messin aboot wi some o the lads fae the team – it wis aboot nine month ago. We goes up tae this wee shoap tae get a coupla cans an stuff an she wis sittin oan a wa' wi some o her pals, an Ah looked at her an ma mooth went aw sorta dry an ma hert sterts bumpin. Ah thought Ah wis gettin the flu or somethin. An wur aw talkin tae them an that an Ah ends up ower sittin on the wa' aside her. Ah say 'talkin', but sumdy's glued ma tongue tae the roof a ma mooth. In fact, it's no' even *ma* tongue, it feels like it's sumdy else's, an it's a coupla sizes too big. Ah couldnae get ma words oot, she musta thocht Ah wis daft or sumthin. Jaz, as usual, isnae havin ony problems. He's goat aw the patter an aw the moves an three lassies hingin oan every word. The way they lassies is actin Ah'm wonderin if Jaz'll be able tae get his big heid through the door when he gets hame.

But Ellen's no' lookin at Jaz, it's *me* she's lookin at, an Ah, weel, Ah'm fa'in in love. Ah'm talkin a loada rubbish an showin aff an daein ma best tae impress her. An it seems tae be workin. We wur gettin oan real brilliant, an every time Ah looked at her the mair beautiful she seemed tae get. The night widda bin perfect if it wisnae fur wan thing: ower her shooder Ah could see Jaz giein us these real funny looks, as if he wis tryin tae tell us sumthin. They three lassies ur still staunin roon him gigglin, but his mind's no' oan them. Efter a while he comes ower tae us an he's giein it this 'Craigie – we goat tae be goin' stuff. Ah didnae want tae go onywhere, but he's goin oan an oan. Finally Ah says 'Right – jist gies a minnit!' Ah arrange tae meet Ellen the next night up at the Wee Park, an she seems dead keen an Ah feel brilliant. Jaz grabs us by the elbow an huckles us doon the road. Ah says 'Whit is it? Whit's aw yon we goat tae be goin stuff? It's no' even hauf nine! Since when wur *you* in a hurry tae get hame?' So then he sterts aw this stuff aboot Ellen, weel, no' sae much aboot Ellen, mair aboot her big brers.

'V'yoo no' heard o the McGill Brers, Craigie, Ellen's big brers? Cleaver an Banjo?'

Ah mindit hearin aboot them, but Ah couldnae mind whit fur.

'Yon's total heidcases, Craigie. Total bams. Drugs an aw yon stuff, real vicious tae. Ther supposed tae a stabbt yon wee guy McNulty – mind a yon? Craigie – ye don' want *onythin* tae dae wi the McGills, Ah'm tellin ye. Ye don' want tae go near ony o them.'

Ye ken aw yon stuff aboot 'love is blind' an aw that keech? It's true an aw. Ah could hear whit Jaz wis tellin us an it aw made sense, sorta, but Ah kent Ah'd nae intention o takin his advice. Aw a could think o wis goin up ther tae see her again. Look – see when Ah'm tellin ye aw this, Ah'm gonnae miss oot a lot o the details, aw the kissin bits an stuff, an me an Ellen up the park an that . . . well . . . it's a bit . . . embarrasin . . . an it's kinna . . . personal like. Yeez widnae be interested onyway, so Ah'll spare ye aw they bits . . . But we goat oan real guid. This wis aw new tae me. A lotta the time we jist talked aboot ord'nary things, like. Ah mind askin her – innocent like – if she'd ony brers or sisters.

'Aye' she says. 'Ah've twa big brers, James an Alastair,' giein them thur Sunday names, like.

Ah nearly says 'Whit wan's Cleaver an whit wan's Banjo?', but Ah stoapt masel in time.

'Whit ur they like?' Ah says.

'Aw ther great' she says. 'They'd dae onythin fur us. See if sumdy messed us aboot like . . . '

An' she's lookin at us funny like when she says this, an Ah feels a wee cauld shiver runnin up ma back, but Ah jist shrugs it aff an . . . naw, Ah said Ah wisnae gonnae gie ye the personal details.

Jaz wis never aff ma case.

'Ah wis talkin tae big Tam Melville,' he says. 'Aboot they McGills. Ah'm tellin ye, Craigie – ther bad news. The worst. Ther no' jist usin aw sorta stuff, ther dealin an aw. You name it an the McGills'll sell ye it. An see if ye owe them an ye cannae pay . . . Tam says he kens a boy Banjo took a sword tae, whit a mess he wis, Craigie.'

'Bit whit's that goat tae dae wi me, Jaz? It's no' Banjo Ah'm seein . . . '

'See that Ellen, Craigie – ye want tae watch her. Ah mean, she kin seem that nice an that, but . . . '

Ah says 'Whit *is* it wi you, Jaz? Ah don' go oan when *you're* seein a lassie, dae Ah?'

An he says 'Look, Craigie, *sumdy's* goat tae look efter ye if yiv no' the sense tae look efter yersel.'

Tae *me*! Talkin tae *me* as if Ah wis daft or sumthin! Ah wisnae tae polite tae him, Ah kin tell ye!

He says 'Onyway, yer no' gaun tae be much use tae the fitba team wi an airm hingin aff or yer kneecaps done in, ur ye?' An he's aff doon the road leavin us staunin.

But Ah'm no' stupit, an some o whit he said did kinna sink in. Like when Ellen says tae us 'J'ye want tae come back tae ma hoose? It's jist ma brers that's in . . . ' Ah made ma excuses. But love's an amazin feelin, an Ah jist seemed tae go fae day tae day waitin tae see her. Ah even stertit washin mair often an buyin deodorants an that. Ma Maw kept giein us these funny looks. Ma Faither didnae say onythin, he jist hud this wee smile. But back tae yon 'love is blind' stuff, Ah huv tae admit, lookin back, ther wis a coupla things that shoulda bothert me mair. Wan wis yon time up at the Wee Park when she wis actin aw funny, like, gigglin too much an jist kinna strange. Thur wisnae a smella drink aff her, bit she wisnae right like. Wan minnit she's laughin an cairyin oan an the next she's gaun tae sleep oan the grass. But Ah didnae let masel think too much aboot it, Ah jist let it go . . . Anither time wis this time wur staunin in this wee lane jist roon fae the chippie an she says 'Ah'm glad yer nice tae me, Craigie. Alastair wis sayin tae me the ither night, "See if emdy ever gies ma wee sister any hassle, Ah'll . . . "' Weel, Ah'll leave the rest tae yer imagination, but it wisnae very nice, Ah kin tell ye. Ah tellt Jaz whit she said, fur he wis talkin tae us again by then, an he goes aw quiet an thoughtfu' like, ye ken yon way he goes. Ah probly shouldnae a tellt him. Strangely enough, efter that he seemed tae stoap giein us aw they warnins aboot the McGills. He hardly mentioned them. But wi Jaz ye kin never ken whit's goin oan deep in his heid.

No' long efter, a coupla things happened. At the time Ah didnae ken whit tae think. First ther wis aw these rumours. Grantie fae the fitba team cams up tae us wan day efter trainin, an he's giein it 'Hey, Craigie, Ah saw yon lassie a yours up the estate last night wi a boy – you no' gaun oot wi her ony mair then?'

Ah jist ignored it. Ah mean, Grantie's aff his heid. An then a lassie in school, Helen Scoular – Ah hardly ken her even – she comes up tae us an says 'See Ellen McGill, Ah heard she's gaun oot wi sumdy else, Craigie.

Ye want tae watch that yin.'

Ah didnae ken whit tae dae. If Ah asked her straight she might pack us in like. Ah felt terrible. Ma Maw wis giein it aw yon 'Whit's up wi your face' stuff, an that jist made it worse. When Ellen wis wi me she seemed the same, but things didnae *feel* the same.

The ither thing wis aw they mix-ups ower when Ah wis meetin her. Jaz cam roon wan day efter school, he says 'Ah bumped intae Ellen when Ah wis daein ma papers, she says she cannae make it fur seeven – kin ye make it eight instead. Ah says Ah'd tell ye. At least Ah think it wis eight she said . . . ' So ther Ah am, strollin up tae the Wee Park at eight an she's no' ther. Ther's these ither lassies ther an Ah says 'Ony o yiz seen Ellen McGill?' an wan says 'Aye, she wis here aboot hauf an oor ago. Ur you the guy that stood her up? She wis pure bealin, so she wis . . . ' We goat that wan sortit oot, but it wisnae easy, ken. She said she'd never met Jaz yon day, never mind tellin him tae gie us a message. Ah tellt her Ah believed her, but Ah didnae really. Ah mean, why wid Jaz a made up sumthin like that? It didnae mak ony sense.

Bit yon wis no' long sortit oot when ther wis the phone call. Ah goes in wan day an ma Maw says, 'A lassie cried Ellen phoned ye. She says tae tell ye she has tae stay in the night. Soundit quite a nice lassie . . . '

Ah mean, it didnae sound right, Ellen never phoned us at hame, but at the time Ah jist acceptit it an went furra gemme a fitba instead. We played that night until we wis aw totally knackered. Wur sittin aboot oan the grass efter, jist talkin like an gettin some Irn Bru doon us, an some o the boys stert talkin aboot Banjo. Andy's goin 'See yon Banjo McGill – did yiz hear aboot it? The polis are efter him – he done some guy wi a blade. Ma faither says aw ther neighbours is signin a petition tae get them moved, him an Cleaver's bin breakin intae ther hooses. An that lassie's . . . ' An then he shuts up, as if he's suddenly remembered Ah'm ther, an they aw stert talkin aboot sumthin else. Aw except Jaz, that is. He's jist sittin kinda quiet.

Some things are awfy hard tae take. Ah goes up the next night tae see if Ah kin see Ellen. These lassies ootside the chippie aw drap ther voices when they see us, an ther lookin at us like. Then wan o Ellen's pals cams ower tae us an gies us this note:

'That's fae Ellen, Craigie,' she says, an gies us this sorta, Ah dunno, *sad* look. Ah opens the note up an reads it. Some o it's a bit kinna . . . personal like. Ah'll no' tell ye everythin she said, cos that's ma ain business, but basically she's gaun oan aboot me staunin her up an stories she's heard aboot me an anither lassie, an if Ah ever go near her again her big brers'll be efter me an stuff like that. Ah foldit it up an pit it in ma poaket – Ah've still goat it in ma bedroom – an Ah jist walked away. Ah tried tae be cool aboot it but Ah didnae manage aw that weel. Ah went hame an . . . weel, it took me a while tae get ower it like. Jaz an the boys wis a help ken, draggin us oot the hoose tae play fitba an go intae toon an have a laugh an that, but it wisnae easy.

Ah've no' seen Ellen fur ages. Ah goat tellt Banjo wis in jile, an the femily wis movin, an ther wis a story that Ellen wis gettin taken intae care, but Ah dinnae ken how much o it wis true. Aw Jaz ever says is 'Craigie – yer better aff wi'oot her. Ther's plenty mair lassies oot ther jist waitin fur ye.' An Ah sometimes wunner if Jaz wis up tae somethin – he kin be awfa fly. Ther wis a lotta things aboot me an Ellen brekkin up that Ah jist didnae unnerstaun, an a coupla times Ah wunnert if this wis wan o Jaz's plans. But naw, Ah don' think he wid dae that tae us.

Wid he?

Iain Mills

I Want To Be Like Henrik Larsson

Henrik Larsson is GORGEOUS.

Henrik comes from Sweden.
They do things differently in Scandinavia,
Says in this star profile they're not so repressed.
Can't imagine Mark Burchill or Barry Ferguson with
   dreads,
Can't imagine either of them naked.
Bet all Scottish footballers wear pyjamas in bed,
Get their hair cut with Grandma's best pudding basin,
Sport velvet slippers after removing poncy club blazers,
Call the manager the archaic title 'Gaffer.'
Henrik: He's clearly something quite different.

So what a shock, what a surprise,
Three years in Scotland and Henrik's succumbed,
Shaved off his beautiful golden tresses.
Not forgetting the man broke his leg badly,

Am I the only one to think his form blighted?
He's scoring goals for fun, but where's the magic gone?
Samson shorn of symbolic strength.

Cantona had his trademark turned up collar,
Petit his ponytail, Vialli's bald heid,
Henrik shaving his locks, that's peer pressure,
Conforming to environmental expectations,
Like taking smack because you bide on a scheme,
Sipping Irn Bru to confirm you're Scottish.

I want to be like Henrik Larsson,
God, I really do.
Parking my Ferrari down at the training ground,
Greeted by fawning middle aged lackeys:
'Hey, it's THE man!'
(Rather, 'THE woman', ye ken what I mean?)

My magical sponsored boots –
Cleaned by spotty trainee laddies:
'Did ye no' see the goal she scored wi' this right foot?
It wus a peach. Aye, she's some lassie.'

I want agents begging me to sign,
Crawling and squirming for their 15%,
My clothes – every one a brand name design.
'Smile at the camera, Helen doll.
That's cool. Off to Troon for the golfing shoot?'

'Not really my scene, man,' I say to the press. As you
     do.

Instead of waltzing around the Glasgow bars,
I'll fly down to London, Paris and New York,
Modelling cheap perfume and comfy sports bras,
That's me in the shampoo ad,
The replacement of the replacement of David Ginola.
And what do you know?
The first female football star on 'The Kirsty Wark
     Show',
The first female professional in the men's beautiful
     game.
Helen Lawson: Glasgow Celtic and Scotland, no less.
No think it will ever happen?
Not so long ago Rangers would not play a Catholic.
Lorenzo Amoruso: Now that's progress.
Fillies have won many a Derby, ask my Ma.

O.k. so I may be a wee bit overweight,
And never amount to very much height,
Bremner and Johnstone were famously small,
Even Henrik probably went through a porky phase.
Footballers found in all shapes and sizes,
I'll not be put off by what's been decided,
By what's always been the masculine score.

I'm training hard, morning, noon, evening and night,
Kicking the ball against the neighbour's side wall.
It's still the way to make the grade,
Despite the talk of coaches with badges,
Technical Directors larging it in Largs –
A new league on the planet Mars.
Real footballers come from the streets, says my Dad,
Rebuild the tenement slums and Scotland will win the
    World Cup.

Ah dinnae ken aboot that.

With ten Henrik Larssons from Sweden maybe,

Ten Henrik Larssons,

Ten Henrik Larssons and ME!

Oh, I wish he'd bring back his blessed cool dreads.

I suppose that's Henrik's prerogative.

Julian Colton